ANDROID
IN THE
ATTIC

NICHOLAS ALLAN

*Hodder
Children's
Books*

A division of Hachette Children's Books

Text and illustrations copyright © 2013 Nicholas Allan

First published in Great Britain in 2013
by Hodder Children's Books

The right of Nicholas Allan to be identified as the Author and
Illustrator of the Work has been asserted by him in accordance with
the Copyright, Designs and Patents Act 1988

1

A Catalogue record for this book is available
from the British Library

ISBN 978 0 340 99706 2

Typeset and designed by Katie Everson

Printed and bound by
CPI Group (UK) Ltd, Croydon, CR0 4YY

The paper and board used in this paperback by Hodder Children's Books
are natural recyclable products made from wood grown in sustainable forests.
The manufacturing processes conform to the environmental regulations
of the country of origin.

Hodder Children's Books
a division of Hachette Children's Books
338 Euston Road, London NW1 3BH
An Hachette UK company
www.hachette.co.uk

 **1**

Aunt Edna's Secret

Billy and Alfie first met their weird Aunt Edna after their mum and dad got run over by a combine harvester.

It had happened one afternoon on holiday. Alfie and Billy were sitting on a gate whilst their parents stood in a field of corn explaining how modern machinery had made farming so much easier.

'The combine-harvester,' their dad had said, 'cuts the corn, turns it into bales, and even ties the bales up. It saves so much time!'

What their mum and dad hadn't realized was that the farmers had saved even more time by hiring two combine-harvesters. As they watched one sweeping across the field a short distance

away, another approached, unnoticed, from over the hill. By the time Alfie and Billy saw it, it was too late. The two children were orphans.

'Orphans? What're they?'

'Us,' said Alfie sadly. 'People who don't have a mum and dad.'

'But you *do* have an aunt,' said the nice lady from the orphanage. 'Professor Edna Stepford, the world-famous scientist.'

It depended, Billy thought, what you meant by an aunt. If an aunt was someone who sent you birthday money and Christmas money and sometimes holiday money and half-term money, then Aunt Edna wasn't an aunt. If an aunt was someone you'd never met, who never sent Christmas cards, who was some kind of weird scientist who hardly left her house, then, yes, they had an aunt.

'Many orphans have no relatives at all. You don't know how lucky you are!' were the last words the nice lady said as they were driven off to their new home.

59 Screw Drive was a thin, sallow, mean-faced house. When the door opened it was no surprise

to be met by a thin, sallow, mean-faced aunt with eyes the colour of glacier ice – a cold, watery blue. These eyes stared at them as if they were very small aliens – or very small laboratory mice.

'You must be Alfie.'

'No, I'm Billy. She's Alfie.'

'I'm Alfie,' said Alfie.

The house seemed normal enough, if a little bare. There were no family photos on the mantelpiece, no books, no cupboards with doors that wouldn't close because they were crammed full of toys. The tables and chairs had spindly metal legs and hard seats. The carpets were fog-grey. The walls were as white as Aunt Edna's lab coat. There wasn't even a television.

'This is awful,' whispered Billy after the first week, lying in bed in the dark of the attic room. He had to whisper. If he spoke any louder he'd activate the sound-sensor on the ceiling which sprayed them both with icy water. This was a device recently invented by their aunt.

'I can't be expected to wake you up, get your meals and organize your lives when I have so much **VERY IMPORTANT WORK** to do,' their aunt had said after a few days of waking them up, getting their meals and organizing their lives.

'Mum and Dad did,' said Alfie.

'And look what happened to them, Elfid,' Aunt Edna said. 'Ended up in little pieces, didn't they? Well, that's not going to happen to me!'

And so their aunt had spent most of the time that first week down in her basement laboratory inventing the following machines to help her:

1. The Masterchef Machine, which cooked up lengths of grey, wet sausage. It had all the right nutrients, but was entirely lacking in taste.

2. The Catapult Bed, which tipped Alfie and Billy out of their beds like cans from a vending machine when the alarm clock rang.

3. The Wheel, a giant, slowly-spinning hamster wheel which forced Alfie and Billy to go for long weekend walks in their backyard.

THE MASTERCHEF MACHINE

THE CATAPULT BED

THE WHEEL

'This is awful,' said Billy.

'It's inhuman,' said Alfie.

'She isn't human,' Billy moaned.

It's interesting that Billy should have mentioned this as that very evening their aunt was inventing something special…

As if things weren't bad enough, Aunt Edna happened to live next door to Mr Snugbug and Justin, his son, who happened to be *the most spoilt child in the world*. Every evening Billy and Alfie

looked down from the tiny attic window into their neighbour's kitchen and saw Justin scoffing dripping pizzas and towering ice-creams. That evening it was chocolate gateau.

Despite the Masterchef Machine, or because of it, Billy and Alfie were always starving. The sight of Justin Snugbug reminded them how hungry they were. They felt like the tramp who was, at that moment, searching for scraps in Aunt Edna's rubbish bin.

'He won't have much luck there,' moaned Billy. 'Aunt Edna's bins are the last place I'd look for food.'

'He doesn't seem to be looking for food,' Alfie said, 'he seems to be collecting scraps of paper.'

'Wow! He *must* be hungry!'

They looked back at Justin, who was finishing off with a couple of Mars bars – and a burp, which they heard even from the attic.

The sight of the chocolate bars reminded them of the huge tin of Cheeki Choko Cherry Cakes Aunt Edna kept in the kitchen. These were for herself for when she was working. It was Billy's idea to raid the tin and it was this that led to the discovery that would change their lives.

'Is this a good idea?' Alfie said.

'Of course it is! I thought of it. Come on!'

Aunt Edna worked in her laboratory unusually late that night. At last they heard her footsteps on the stairs. As soon as she closed the door of her bedroom, Billy started across the landing. Alfie grabbed his arm and pulled him back.

'Don't be such a scaredy cat,' Billy whispered impatiently.

Alfie said nothing, but pointed to little square plugs along each wall of the landing. 'Laser-sensors,' she whispered.

'How do you know?'

'Read about them in a book.'

After the sensors, Alfie noticed a trip-wire on the top step. Soon it was Alfie leading the way. They made it to the kitchen, but when they switched on the light they got the shock of their lives.

Standing before them, staring straight at them, was Aunt Edna!

'Aargh!' cried Billy, hiding behind Alfie.

'It can't be,' whispered Alfie.

'It is,' said their aunt. 'And what, Alfie, do you think you and your brother are doing here?'

That's weird, thought Alfie. It was only the second time Aunt Edna had got her name right. Even more weird, her eyes had turned brown.

Just as Alfie noticed this, the kitchen door flew open.

Spinning round, Billy and Alfie found themselves staring directly into the ice-blue eyes of their aunt.

'Aargh!' cried Billy, trying to decide which side of Alfie to hide behind.

The two children looked from one aunt to the other. It was like a nightmare in stereo.

'And what, Alison, are you and your brother doing here?'

So at least Alfie could tell this was the real Aunt Edna. But who – or what – was the other?

'We … we…' began Billy.

'Never mind,' said Aunt Edna, dismissing him. 'You may as well meet your new Aunt Android. She'll be living with you in the attic and looking after you from now on. She's faster than me, stronger than me, and not nearly so nice. And one more thing…' The blue eyes burned into them. 'Don't try to creep down here again to steal my Choko Cakes. Your new aunt will be watching you. She will always be watching you. Because,' she said darkly, 'androids never sleep.'

The Case of the Cheeki Choko Cherry Cakes

When Billy and Alfie had been at their new school for eight weeks, Mrs Portcullis – the headteacher – announced that sports day was in a week's time. That day, the children were given a note for their parents:

PARENTS' CHARITY RACE

Mums and Dads! Uncles, Aunts!
Here's a challenge, here's your chance!
Enter now the charity race
And win your kids
THE CHOKO CAKE CASE!
£4 entry fee

At the end of the day the children rushed out to bully their mums and dads into immediate training. But there was one person who couldn't be bullied. By now everyone had become used to seeing the tall, thin figure in the dirty white coat marching Billy and Alfie to the school gates in the morning and marching them back at the end of the day.

'Regular as clockwork,' they said, not realizing, that they'd more or less hit the nail on the head. Aunt Android was nothing but plastic, metal and the electronic circuits from ten iPods, a handful of mobiles and an old washing machine.

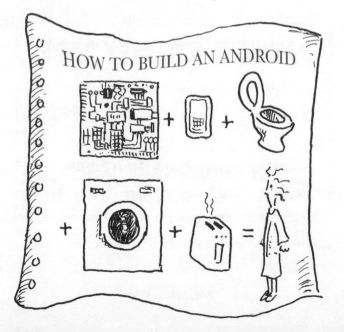

HOW TO BUILD AN ANDROID

'Your aunt hasn't a chance,' said Justin Snugbug. 'She's never done a bit of exercise in her life. She's got about as much chance of winning the race as … as … as a washing machine!'

The next morning, looking out of their bedroom window, Billy and Alfie saw Mr Snugbug in white sports-gear running and puffing his way round the block. Soon he was joined by other mums, dads, aunts, uncles and near-relatives, similarly dressed, similarly red-faced.

As they watched, a supermarket van drew up outside 59 Screw Drive with two men inside.

'A delivery!' said Billy in disbelief. 'Food! Real food! Aunt Edna's realized we're human after all.'

They watched one of the delivery men walking towards the house.

Opening their door, they crept down the stairs as the bell rang.

'I didn't order any food.' Aunt Edna was saying. 'We certainly don't need any food in this house!'

'Isn't that the man who was going through the dustbins?' Alfie whispered to Billy.

'Why would he be going through our bins if he works at the supermarket?'

'Perhaps he only does that in his spare time. Strange ear he's got. It's made of tin.'

'If I could ask you to come out to the van so you can sign a cancellation form, Professor...'

'I've got better things to do than sign cancellation forms. I'm a scientist,' said a furious Aunt Edna and slammed the door in his face.

Alfie and Billy went back to their room. As the van disappeared the driver looked up. He was a thin man with something odd about his face which made Alfie look again, but he was gone.

'Did you see the driver?' she asked. But Billy was sitting on his bed thinking of food.

* * *

When Billy had shown the real Aunt Edna the
sports day letter she'd immediately torn it up.

'As if!' she said simply.

Billy would've forgotten about the race
altogether but, two days later, he and Alfie
discovered an amazing secret about Aunt
Android that made them think again. It was Mr
Snugbug, of all people, who helped them make
the discovery.

That morning, Billy and Alfie were marched
out of the house as usual. Just as they reached
the end of their road, Mr Snugbug appeared
round the corner in his white shorts, T-shirt and
trainers and accidentally stamped hard on Aunt
Android's foot.

Something very weird happened.

Aunt Android didn't yell out or faint with pain.

That wasn't weird. She was an android.

What was weird was that she smiled.

It wasn't a sneery, nasty little smile, not the sort of smile Aunt Edna used after she'd invented a pair of electrified underpants or a chocolate bar that bit back.

No, it was a kind smile.

Aunt Android stood quite still, as if her batteries had run out … or as if she was waiting for something.

'Should we go, then?' said Billy.

'Where would you like to go?' asked Aunt Android.

'Well, we have to go to school,' said Billy, looking at her curiously.

'School? That doesn't sound much like fun,' she said with the same smile on her face. 'I can think of much better places to go. I can offer a list of 3,705 better places to go. Only one worse place to go – prison.'

'Two worse places,' Billy corrected her. 'You've forgotten 59 Screw Drive.'

'Besides, we have to go to school,' said Alfie.

'Have to? Oh, well,' answered Aunt Android sadly, 'if you have to. I suppose I can only obey.'

The android turned in the direction of the school and walked on. Billy and Alfie followed.

'What's happened?' Billy whispered.

'Mr Snugbug stamped on her foot. That's what happened.'

Alfie thought about this. By the time they reached the school gate, she was ready to try out a scientific experiment.

'Aunt Android?'

'Yes?'

'Would you give Billy and me our sweet money now?'

They knew Aunt Android

carried change in her pocket in case of emergencies. She removed two one-pound coins and gave one to each of them.

'Wow!' said Billy, accepting the coin.

Alfie, daring to experiment just that little bit further, said, 'Sweets are very expensive these days.'

Two more coins dropped into their hands.

'Wow!' said Billy again. He was so surprised that he let his schoolbag drop to the floor. It fell heavily on Aunt Android's foot. Immediately, her smile faded. 'Why are you still standing here?' she demanded, pointing at the school gate. 'Get inside this instant.'

Then she spun round sharply and marched away.

Two days before the sports day race was to take place, Alfie was planning.

'When Mr Snugbug stamped on her foot, she suddenly became friendly.' She and Billy were whispering in the dark again. 'She did what we wanted. And when you dropped your bag on her—'

'She went back to normal.'

'Perhaps if we stamped on her foot again, she'd go back to being friendly.'

'We could ask her for more sweet money!'

'We could ask for more sweets!'

'Or Cheeki Choko Cherry Cakes. Let's go and do it now! Come on!'

'No, Billy! We've got to keep it a secret.'

'But Choko Cakes, Alfie. We could have a whole case of them, like the sports day race prize!'

'The prize…' Alfie thought a bit more. 'I'd forgotten about that. Imagine how many cakes there must be in that case!' Then she said, 'Maybe we could win it!'

'Aunt Edna would have to go in for the race, and Aunt Edna would never go in for it,' said Billy.

'But Aunt Android could win it!' said Alfie.

'But Aunt Edna wouldn't let Aunt Android enter.'

'No, she wouldn't…'

'Well, then, what are you talking about?'

'Give me your two pounds, Billy.'

'No way.'

'I know how we can win the prize.'

'How?'

'By you giving me your two pounds.'

'You'd better have a good idea then.'

So Alfie told him her idea.

Because many of the parents had to go to work, the sports day race was held first thing in the morning. In fact, many of the mums and dads arrived in their sports gear, including, of course, Mr Snugbug. They limbered up on the sports-field, even as the dew was drying on the short, summer grass.

When Aunt Android arrived with Billy and Alfie they were directed by Miss Sprint, the sports teacher, up onto the field, where the other parents were lining up.

Among the remainder of grandparents and babies in the audience, Alfie noticed a thin man in a black coat with something strange about his face, something absent. It was like a cartoon face with just enough lines to make it look like a face.

'It's the delivery van driver!' Alfie nudged Billy.

'Eh?'

'That man with the weird face.'

'Alfie, just concentrate on what we've got to do,' said Billy, whose own concentration powers were at their best when he was doing something naughty.

Justin Snugbug watched as Aunt Android approached.

'Just in time!' jeered Justin to no one in particular. She won't even make it to the starting line!'

Mr Snugbug grinned too as he jogged on the spot.

'Welcome to our sports day,' announced

Mrs Portcullis. 'And now ... straight to our first event – the grown-up's charity race. Remember, a special Cheeki Choko Cherry Cake Case goes to the lucky children of the winner! Competitors, are you ready? On your marks ... get set—'

At this point, Billy stamped hard on Aunt Android's shoe.

'Go!' cried the headteacher, and everyone but Aunt Android ran.

'Run!' screamed Billy. 'Run, you stupid machine! Run!'

'It's time for me to return home,' Aunt Android said. Billy stamped on her foot again. Still nothing happened.

Suddenly, Alfie realized what was wrong and stamped on the other foot.

'Give me a bead on that winning-post!' Aunt Android beamed and shot off, her thin legs blurring like a circular-saw.

Within seconds she'd caught up with the stragglers. The runners became aware of a sudden draft and the flap of a white laboratory coat before a thin figure flew past them and out of sight.

'Burn that oil!' shouted Billy.

Aunt Android was beginning the second lap and soon overtook a gasping Mr Snugbug. He couldn't believe it.

Justin couldn't believe it either.

'Come on, you stupid parent!' he shouted when he saw his dad staggering with exhaustion. 'Don't just stand there. We need those Cheeki Choko Cherry Cakes. Move it!'

But his dad could go no further.

Justin had noticed how Alfie had got her aunt going and an idea began to form in his brain.

This'll do the trick, he thought, and he stamped as hard as he could on his dad's toes.

'Aargh!' Mr Snugbug howled, and collapsed onto the grass. Just in time to see Aunt Android cross the finishing line.

Twenty minutes before this, Aunt Edna was sitting deep in her laboratory sharpening a wasp's tail with a micro-laser, when she noticed her android hadn't returned. Aunt Edna could tell the time by Aunt Android. She was as regular as a washing-cycle.

'Something must have happened.' She bit impatiently into a Cheeki Choko Cherry Cake. 'Bother!'

Reluctantly, she turned off the laser and scurried off to the school.

Back at the sports field, Billy had succeeded in stamping on Aunt Android's foot a final time. The android froze immediately, then spun round. 'I must return home at once.' She walked rapidly from the field and out of the school, narrowly missing the searching gaze of Aunt Edna.

When Aunt Edna arrived at school, the secretary directed her to the playing field. She could hear the cheering as she approached.

'And now,' announced the headteacher, before an enormous case standing on the grass. 'For their aunt's triumphant run, may I present Billy and Alfie with this magnificent and well-deserved prize.'

'Cheat! Cheat!' shouted Justin Snugbug. 'Their aunt's a cheat!'

There were gasps and stares and Justin noticed that Aunt Edna was only a step away from him.

'I'll prove it!' he shouted, pointing at her. He stamped as hard as he could on her foot.

'Aargh!' cried Aunt Edna, collapsing onto the grass.

Having just experienced the exact same pain as Aunt Edna, from the same culprit, Mr Snugbug chose that moment to do something he'd never done in his life: he told Justin off.

'You … you … unkind boy!' he said before all the parents.

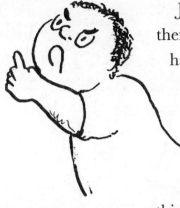

Justin looked shocked, then hurt. He stared hard at his dad.

'Wait until I get you home,' he muttered.

Billy and Alfie were enjoying all this, of course. Nearly as much as they enjoyed collecting the prize.

'Congratulations to Billy and Alfie's aunt!' cheered Mrs Portcullis.

'Hooray!' everyone cried.

Aunt Edna, recovering in the arms of Mr Snugbug, accepted the applause in total confusion but with what looked like the beginnings of a smile on her face. No one had ever been nice to her like this before.

'Gosh,' said Billy, as he and Alfie

walked home that sunny afternoon, carrying the case of Cheeki Choko Cherry Cakes between them, 'Aunt Edna almost looked friendly.'

'Almost … human!' agreed Alfie. 'Almost, for a moment, like Aunt Android!'

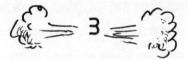

The Atomic Fart-Machine

'**Billy** and Alfie's aunt ran a terrific race!' said Mrs Portcullis a few weeks later. 'So unexpected!'

'Without any training either,' Miss Sprint agreed. 'It just goes to show, don't you think, Floris? Keeping slim makes all the difference.' Neither could have known that Aunt Edna's figure wasn't due to careful eating, but pure meanness.

'I was just thinking…' Miss Sprint continued. 'The children eat so unhealthily and Professor Stepford is a famous scientist. Don't you think, Floris, it would do the children good – not to mention the reputation of the school – if we could get her to give a little talk about healthy eating.'

Although Mrs Portcullis was a bit podgy and not at all keen to be told what food she should be eating, she was very keen on making the school look good.

'Now that is a thought!' she agreed. 'I'll write a letter for Billy to give to his aunt.'

It was then they both heard the third elephant's fart of the day coming from the other side of the staffroom door.

* * *

Life for Billy and Alfie had been transformed since they'd discovered Aunt Android's secret weakness. Billy had thought of all the things that they couldn't do without a grown-up who would pay. This included going to the best films, eating lots of junk food, and even playing the penny-slot machines in arcades.

To do all this they would need *money*! Lots of it. And naturally it was Alfie who thought up the plan to get it.

Every Saturday the two children were sent with Aunt Android to do the weekly shop at the supermarket in the town square. Aunt Edna gave her exactly the right money for the food on the shopping-list. When they returned she checked the amount on the receipt. It meant that they couldn't have bought a Smartie between them without their aunt knowing.

The square was a busy place on a Saturday; street performers had coins and notes sprinkled at them like bread to ducks. There were magicians, musicians, acrobats and, Alfie noticed, mime-artists dressed in gold or grey painted clothes who just stood absolutely still. It seemed ridiculous to be showered with coins for doing nothing. That's when it occurred to her that no one would be better at keeping still than Aunt Android.

'She could do that without blinking,' Alfie said. 'She wouldn't need to blink in a thousand years. Not even if you slapped her in the face.'

'She wouldn't blink if you stuck a white-hot needle in her eye,' agreed Billy. 'But what would be the point?'

'Just wait,' said Alfie.

The following Saturday, Aunt Android was standing still in the middle of the square. Actually, she wasn't standing. 'That's far too easy,' she sneered.

Crowds gathered in no time. They stood gaping, waiting for her to collapse from the strain. Soon they started tossing coins at her, partly in admiration, mostly trying to make her lose her balance. Billy and Alfie quickly gathered the coins in old Cheeki Choko Cherry Cake boxes until they were full. Then, while Aunt Android looked for a taxi home, Billy and Alfie hurried to the toy shop.

The first thing Billy bought was a remote-controlled fart machine.

'Who made that noise?' demanded Mrs Portcullis, stepping out of her room.

The corridor was empty, as it had been the previous two times. The farts seemed to come from nowhere. They'd been going on all week.

'Right!' said Mrs Portcullis, 'Gather all the children into the hall, Petunia.'

The first few farts of the week had been real ones, but electronic ones had now taken their place. Mrs Portcullis wouldn't have considered herself a good headteacher had she not been able to distinguish between the two. It was, in fact, one of the first things she'd been taught at Teacher Training College.

When the school was assembled, Mrs Portcullis demanded which child had in their possession a fart machine.

Dead silence met her ears. Then, quite unexpectedly, the fourth elephant fart of the day erupted from the vicinity of class 4D. A few giggles followed. Mrs Portcullis began to walk towards them. The giggles became uncontrollable

laughter when a bombardment of farts issued from Billy's book-bag. Billy shook the bag wildly but the farts continued.

'Billy Stepford! I might have known! You will go to my office immediately.'

Mrs Portcullis left the stage.

'It was Justin Snugbug,' whispered Billy to Alfie. 'He's got hold of another remote-control.'

Since Aunty Anne (as they now called her) had come under their control, Billy had become much more mischievous. He'd already been in trouble for taking bets on how many teachers he could give his cold to. He'd caused havoc in the classroom with his remote-controlled stink bomb-dropping indoor helicopter. Billy had become more and more popular – and Justin more and more jealous.

'We should get Aunty Anne to deal with him,' Alfie said.

'Yes, electrocute him. That would teach him a lesson.'

'Billy Stepford! Silence!' Miss Sprint approached. 'You're in enough trouble as it is.'

'Breaking wind,' Mrs Portcullis said blandly, as if she was saying, 'Quadratic Equation', 'Environmental issue', or 'Her Majesty, the Queen', 'is not polite – whether from a bottom or a machine. You, Billy, are guilty of both. There is never any need for it. I simply won't tolerate it in this school. I think it is time to speak to your aunt when she comes to give her talk.'

'Talk, Mrs Portcullis?'

The headteacher produced a letter.

'I want you to give this to your aunt. And

make sure it is delivered. I will check.'

'I wish we could open it,' Billy said as they walked home, 'but if we do, Aunt Edna will know.'

'Give that to me, Billy,' said Aunty Anne. 'I think I can help.'

Her eyes glowed green, like luminous paint, and faint rays fell onto the envelope.

'Dear Professor Stepford,' she read. 'We are very privileged to have the nephew and niece of an eminent scientist attend our school. We would be most honoured and grateful if you would agree to talk to the children. The subject we would like you to discuss is nutrition. I will ring you to arrange a time for your visit.

'At a later date I would also like to speak to you about Billy, who requires disciplinary measures…'

Billy looked at his shoes.

'Disciplinary measures, Billy? What have you been up to?' Aunty Anne looked up.

'Farting,' Alfie said.

'But that's what humans do.'

'We know that,' Alfie said, 'but we're not allowed to.'

'Humans are very strange things, aren't they?' she said thoughtfully. 'But don't worry, Billy, I'll sort this out. Easy-queasy.'

Aunty Anne had already worked out that her creator would program her to give the talk. She'd also worked out that Aunt Edna would want to speak to Mrs Portcullis about Billy's behaviour. Sure enough, the talk was to be the following Tuesday after school; the meeting about Billy first thing the morning after.

'We must let everyone know about this, Petunia!' Mrs Portcullis insisted once Aunt Edna had confirmed. 'Call the *Bretford Express*, Petunia. Send invites to all the

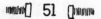

parents, the governors, and the Mayor.'

'Right, Floris!'

Mrs Portcullis sat back, beaming with pleasure. She thought of what sandwiches and cream cakes to include in the special guest's buffet. *I could win a Headteacher's Medal for this!* she thought.

On the evening before the talk, the front page of the *Bretford Express* ran an article.

'Oh look,' said Billy, busy reading the article above. 'Two very dangerous criminals have been seen in the quiet town of Bretford. The police have not yet given details, but MI6 and Interpol have given warning… Wow! You don't think they mean us? For tricking people into giving us money?'

'Yes, probably, Billy, and for being in possession of a fart machine and using it with undue care.'

Even Billy had to laugh.

Later that night, after they had eaten their usual supper, they watched Aunty Anne recharging in her chair and downloading Aunt Edna's speech into her computer.

'I wonder what Aunty Anne's planned?' Alfie whispered to Billy, as they lay in the darkness.

Something that will liven up the Bretford Express, was all she'd been willing to tell them.

'I don't know,' said Billy. 'But it had better be something brilliant. If Aunt Edna has her meeting with Mrs Portcullis, I'll probably never eat again!'

Since receiving the letter from the headteacher,

Aunt Edna's eyes had been particularly icy, and Billy had been deprived of half his evening grey sausage.

Lying in bed, the two children tried to imagine what life would have been like if Aunty Anne hadn't come into existence. But no one, not even Aunt Edna, could have guessed how unforgettable and life-saving Aunty Anne's speech would turn out to be.

On the day of the talk, the children assembled in the hall with their parents: the front-row seating was reserved for the Mayor and other officials, and, of course, the *Bretford Express* photographer.

The special guests were – at that moment – enjoying coffee, little sausages, ham sandwiches and chocolate cream cakes in the staffroom.

Readers of the *Bretford Express* had, from curiosity, come out of their houses to see the famous professor. They watched as Aunty Anne scissor-stepped, down the street towards the school. Billy and Alfie were also watching from the assembly hall window.

As they waited, Alfie spotted the tall, thin delivery van driver again. He was taking a photo of Aunty Anne with his mobile. Again, Alfie

noticed how like a cartoon his face was, with something not quite right ... something missing.

'Billy, it's the van driver again.'

'It's not important, Alfie,' Billy said, 'Concentrate on what we have to do.'

'Fine. Shhhh. She's coming!' whispered Alfie, sitting at the front of the hall.

'Don't muck this up, Alfie,' Billy whispered back.

Everything depended on Alfie's plan. By lucky coincidence, Alfie had won that year's Science Cup. Mrs Portcullis had had the brilliant idea of letting their aunt present the prize before her talk. 'The *Bretford Express* will love that!' she told Miss Sprint.

Once the important guests had settled in their seats, introductions were made, and then the presentation announced.

'Clearly, young Alfie is following in her aunt's footsteps!' Mrs Portcullis laughed generously at her little joke. 'Who knows? Alfie could be the next Marie Curie – or, indeed, Professor Stepford.'

The cup had grown since it was last awarded;

Mrs Portcullis thought a bigger one might show up better in the photo. As Alfie stepped up to receive the cup, she aimed it carefully over Aunty Anne's left foot and dropped it. The photographer's camera flashed. The audience gasped.

'Are you all right, Professor Stepford?' said Mrs Portcullis quickly picking up the cup.

'Oh, perfectly. My feet are made of steel.'

'It's all that healthy eating, ha, ha!' laughed Mrs Portcullis, as she pushed Alfie off the stage. 'And now! Mayor, Mayoress, governors, ladies and gentlemen, boys and girls – Professor Edna Stepford.'

Aunty Anne stood up and began to talk about vitamins, nutrients, protein, carbohydrates and fats, until the audience settled into a comfortable afternoon doze.

After about half an hour, she said, 'To conclude with the most important part of my talk, I'd like you all to think about what the body throws away.' This made the children sit up. 'The body must be able to get rid of its waste easily and quickly, *so we must never be stopped from going to the lavatory.* We must also never prevent the poisonous gases from escaping... This is done, very simply by farting. Allow me to demonstrate.'

Aunty Anne pushed out her bottom and let

off a supersonic fart. It resounded through the hall like sudden thunder. The speakers vibrated. The microphone wobbled. The audience, now wide-awake, gasped, and the Mayor's face turned green.

Mrs Portcullis's face had turned a strange puce colour.

It didn't stop there.

Aunty Anne demonstrated the:

Cow-moo fart   ballerina fart   musical fart

tyrannosaurus fart   underwater fart

granny fart   Coke fart   Top secret fart

dynamite fart

curry tart

flower fairy fart

1000cc motorbike fart

Let's party farty

red-hot screaming mega-
neutron toxic bomb fart.

When she was finished, a deafening silence filled the hall.

'And that,' said Aunty Anne, 'concludes my talk on healthy eating. Thank you.' She sat down.

For a moment the silence resumed and then, as instructed, Justin Snugbug stood up to thank the speaker with some specially prepared words, now wishing he hadn't been picked.

'Thank you, Professor Stepford, for this wonderful talk,' he began. 'We now know what we must do, and we shall make sure we do it as much as possible.'

The children started to titter and some of the parents too.

'But not only that, we should make sure that everyone knows about it by doing it loud and clear.'

Now even the Mayor was grinning.

Justin's cheeks turned crimson; he hesitated to end his speech. 'And I know I will do it – at home and at school – and know my body will be much better for it!'

The line of special guests joined the audience in uncontrollable giggling as Justin, sweating in embarrassment, sat down.

As they left the hall, Mrs Portcullis leant over to the school secretary.

'That appointment with Professor Stepford about Billy's bad behaviour?'

'Yes, Mrs Portcullis?'

'Cancel it.'

'You must be the best fart-machine in the world.' said Billy as the three walked home afterwards.

'I'm the best machine in the world,' Aunty Anne said.

'You're the best aunt in the world,'

said Alfie, and took her metal-cold hand and leaned against her.

Just as she said this, a large black car with blacked-out windows drew up at the kerb and two men stepped out. One of them was a tall, thin man with a cartoon-like pebble-shaped face. The other was the delivery van driver. Alfie noticed his right hand stuck out like a sore thumb – it seemed to be made of metal too.

'Look!' said Alfie. 'It's those men again.'

But before she could say anything else, the two men grabbed Aunty Anne and forced her into the back of the car. The door slammed shut;

the engine revved. Then, just as suddenly, the doors opened, the two men jumped out and ran, gasping heavily, down the street.

Aunty Anne stepped calmly out of the car and Alfie and Billy caught the faintest whiff of hell's toilets and elephant houses and gorillas' underpants. 'Most fortunate, that talk,' Aunty Anne said. 'It reminded me of the many uses of the fart. Well, we may as well drive home. Jump in.'

On the way back Billy and Alfie questioned Aunty Anne about the men but, for once, she had no answers.

Back in their room that night, the children

agreed that, whatever happened, they would protect Aunty Anne as if she were their very own mum!

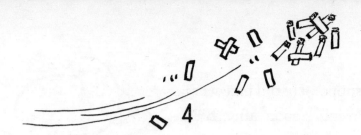

4

Unidentified Flying Cheeseburgers

'**Tomato** and mozzarella pizza … chips…'

'What about pudding?'

'Looks like … chocolate cake with whipped cream.'

'He had that yesterday.'

'Yesterday it was with vanilla and peppermint ice-cream.'

Billy gazed through the lenses of the new binoculars he'd bought that Saturday with Aunty Anne's town square performance money. Mr Snugbug was serving up Justin's

supper. He did this every
evening soon after Billy
and Alfie had finished
theirs and been sent to bed. Despite the extra
money, their main meals were still the grey
sausages prepared by the Masterchef Machine.

'I'd like a dad who cooked proper food every
evening.'

'I'd like a proper a dad,' said Alfie, lying on
her bed.

'At least we've got Aunty Anne.'

'Do you think Aunt Edna would like a
husband?' Alfie asked brightly.

'No,' said Billy with complete certainty.

'No, you're right,' said Alfie. 'But did you
see the way she looked at Mr Snugbug when he
picked her up at the Charity Race?'

'No.'

'Well, she looked at him strangely. He looked
at her too.'

'Everyone looks at her. She's a sight.'

'No, but … you know.'

'Perhaps Mr Snugbug's looking for a wife.'

'Who'd marry Aunt Edna?'

'Well, who'd marry Mr Snugbug?'

Justin had finished his pizza and Mr Snugbug was serving the chocolate cake, expertly heated so that whipped cream melted deliciously all over it. It was too much for Billy.

'It's our duty to bring Mr Snugbug and Aunt Edna together,' he said. 'Otherwise we're never going to eat proper food again.'

'But how?'

They pondered this, and then turned to each other.

'Aunty Anne!'

The next morning, on the way to school, Billy instructed Aunty Anne to be friendly to Mr Snugbug.

'Look as if you want to marry him,' Billy advised.

'I've not been programmed for that, Billy,' Aunty Anne said. 'It's not a piece of software your aunt thought to include.'

'Aunt Edna wouldn't know enough about it to

be able to include it,' Alfie said. 'But it's really easy. You just have to make your face look like this.' Alfie stopped in the street and gazed up into the sky as if she was thinking of a chocolate bar.

With her super-computer Aunty Anne was quickly able to copy the look. She tried it out whenever she encountered Mr Snugbug in Screw Drive or when he was watering the garden. In fact she was so successful that a week later, as Billy and Alfie left for school, Mr Snugbug was waiting with Justin outside their house.

'We thought we'd walk with you,' he beamed fatly. 'We both need the exercise – DON'T WE, JUSTIN?'

'That would be lovely, Mr Snugbug,' Aunty Anne looked up at the sky as if she was thinking about a chocolate bar – or a lovely plug-socket in her case.

'Please. Call me Morris ... Edna.'

Justin looked at his dad as if he himself had eaten too many chocolates and was ready to vomit them back over the pavement. As they walked, he listened to the two of them talk and became increasingly worried. The last thing he wanted to do was share his life – or, more accurately, his burgers, chocolate cake and frequent visits to the toy shop – with Billy and Alfie.

* * *

Buried deep in her cellar, Aunt Edna – much like the rats she was training to spy on children – knew little of the life going on above her head. On the occasions she left 59 Screw Drive, when her Cheeki Choko Cherry Cake supplies were low, she sometimes saw her neighbour in the front garden, but they'd never spoken.

She was shocked the first time he smiled and said, 'Lovely morning, Edna.'

Not long after this she received a greater shock. In the post she found a birthday card – the first she'd had since she was little.

To Edna, love from your neighbour Morris

'How did he know it was my birthday?' she wondered.

Aunt Edna sat nervously in her laboratory, with a strange feeling in her stomach. It felt a bit like she'd swallowed a Cheeki Choko Cherry Cake, but warmer and more mysterious.

Then she experienced a shock even greater than the birthday card. At Alfie's suggestion, Mr Snugbug dropped a note through the letterbox of number 59 inviting Aunt Edna out to dinner. Fortunately for Billy and Alfie, Aunt Edna had to give a lecture that night and told the children to tell him. This was their chance.

When Mr Snugbug asked Aunty Anne if she'd got his letter that morning on the way to school, she replied, 'I can think of nothing better,' and looked up at the sky as if thinking of a can of oil.

'But you can't eat food,' Billy said that evening. 'What will you do?'

'Don't worry about that. What do you like?'

'Burgers!'

'Chocolate fudge cake!'

'Ice-cream!'

'Easy-queasy,' she said.

When they arrived home on the afternoon of the big day, Aunt Edna had already left for her lecture. By six-thirty, when Mr Snugbug approached the door with a bunch of roses and a smile, they were prepared. The door was opened by a woman with red hair and a kitchen apron.

'Is Edna ready?'

'I'll tell her you're here. I'm Mrs Bottomly, the babysitter.'

At super-speed, Mrs Bottomly disappeared and within a few minutes Aunt Edna appeared. She didn't look so different from Mrs Bottomly, except for her wild hair. 'Must be a relative,' thought Mr Snugbug.

The first warm evening of the summer turned the pavements

a soft peach colour and filled the garden trees with sleepless finches. Aunty Anne's radar-sensors had anticipated this warmth and she had asked Mr Snugbug to book a table outside. While Mr Snugbug worried if the menu would be healthy enough, Aunty Anne made sure Billy and Alfie were in position behind the rose bush that sat beyond the tables of the other diners.

'What takes your fancy, Edna? I like the look of the … lentil salad, I suppose,' he sighed unhappily.

'A double-cheese burger for me, with a double portion of chips too, thank you,' Aunty Anne answered. 'No lettuce. Heavy on the tomato sauce.'

Mr Snugbug sat stunned. Then with a sigh of relief, he ordered the same. By the time the waitress brought the burgers, Mr Snugbug was so hungry he forgot all about Aunty Anne and buried himself in his food. Aunty Anne's eyes narrowed into

telescopic sights. Her hand flipped her burger and, with the precision of a sniper's rifle, it streaked through the air and landed on the plate Billy was holding in readiness.

'Where're the chips?' Billy complained. 'I ordered double fries!'

A double portion of chips landed on either side of the burger – still steaming hot.

'This is the best burger I've ever tasted, I think,' said Alfie.

'It's also the priciest burger you've ever tasted. This is the most expensive restaurant in town.'

'I bet Snugbug doesn't even bring Justin here.'

'I bet he doesn't bring himself here.'

Shortly after they finished the last chip, a generous wedge of dark chocolate cake, followed by a comet-tail of ice cream landed on another plate. Two triangular wafers stabbed the ice cream like daggers.

'Wow!' said Billy.

'Easy-queasy!' said Alfie.

'I think it's working,' Billy whispered as they set off for school the next morning, watching Mr Snugbug gazing at Aunty Anne as if she were a chocolate bar.

'Yes,' said Alfie. 'The problem is, how is it going to work with Aunt Edna?'

That same morning, however, two weird but helpful things happened at 59 Screw Drive. The first was when the doorbell rang.

Aunt Edna hated interruptions. She was just perfecting a new stink bomb which only children would smell, so it was with reluctance that she climbed the stairs and opened the door.

On the doorstep was a box of chocolates.

Aunt Edna never ate chocolate except for her 2.5 Cheeki Choko Cherry Cakes a day. She went into the kitchen to throw away the box. As usual,

Aunty Anne was sitting in her recharging chair. As Aunt Edna passed, she accidentally trod on the android's left foot. Suddenly, Aunty Anne sang in a soft, sweet voice:

If I were the only girl in the world,
And you were the only boy
Nothing else would matter
in the world todaaaaay...

Aunty Anne's batteries ran down, her eyes glazed red, and the singing slowed to a halt. It was one of the songs Aunty Anne had learned to sing in the town square as part of her Saturday morning act.

Aunt Edna watched the android, transfixed. It was like watching herself singing (something she'd never done in her life) and again she felt that weird feeling in her stomach, like swallowing a Choko Cake, but warmer and more mysterious.

She went back downstairs, absentmindedly taking the chocolates with her. By the end of the afternoon she'd eaten the whole box.

It's difficult to

know how Aunt Edna and Mr Snugbug's next meeting might have gone. But before this could happen, Aunt Edna disappeared completely.

5

Kidnapped

At first Billy and Alfie thought Aunt Edna had gone to a science conference. This was because, when they got home one afternoon, they found a note on the kitchen table which said:

Gone to a science conference.

Back tomorrow evening,

Be good.

Aunt Edna

'A whole day!' said Billy.

'Pizza for supper!' said Alfie.

Next morning, long after Justin and Mr Snugbug had given up ringing Professor Stepford's doorbell and left for school, Alfie and Billy still lay in bed, watching the rays of the early sun turning the grey attic walls a golden-yellow. Only the smell of cooking bacon compelled the two to sit up as Aunty Anne entered with a breakfast tray.

'We're not going to school today, Aunty Anne.' Billy instructed, swallowing a fried egg, his mouth dribbling with melted butter. 'Please phone to say we've got high temperatures.'

'And we need caring treatment,' Alfie added, digging into a hillock of baked beans.

'Very sensible,' Aunty Anne agreed. 'You need time off to broaden your education.'

During the day Billy and Alfie were thoroughly educated in different varieties of food, toys and interesting jewellery for Alfie. Even better for Alfie were the weird books on bridge-building, cheating at cards, cybernetics, archery, black magic, white and turquoise magic, submarines and other books on subjects that she didn't know existed.

At lunchtime Aunty Anne went shopping and returned with bags of choclate biscuits, crisps, popcorn, huge bottles of Coke, comics, teen magazines, a couple of iPods, a DVD player, two cheeseburgers and fries and chocolate milkshakes. The afternoon vanished in a haze of sugary goodness, filled stomachs and Star Wars.

'It's funny,' Billy said, as they lay in bed in the early evening to avoid Aunt Edna's return. 'It's almost good that Aunt Edna's coming back. I really enjoy tricking her with Aunty Anne. It's a bit like being at school,' he added. 'It's almost more fun having school rules, isn't it? So you can break them. In fact, I expect that's why they invented school rules.'

But the next morning Aunt Edna still wasn't back. At breakfast they asked Aunty Anne if she'd left any instructions.

'No instructions. Perhaps you'd better let me see the note she left.'

It was Alfie who had been wise enough to keep the note. Aunty Anne's eyes illuminated the

paper briefly with ultra-violet light.

'Your aunt didn't write this.'

'What?'

'It's fake.'

'Fake? What do you mean, "fake"?' asked Alfie. 'Who else would have written it?'

Aunty Anne's computer did a quick search. 'Whoever it was,' she told them finally, 'has stolen your aunt.'

Aunt Edna never locked the cellar door. She knew she didn't need to because no one would ever dare enter. Even now the children hesitated in front of the heavy wooden door.

'What if she's blown herself up and bits of her are all over the walls and dripping off the ceiling?' Alfie said.

'Just go in,' whispered Billy, pushing her forward.

'No, you go,' whispered Alfie.

'You go,' they both whispered, turning to Aunty Anne.

Aunty Anne stepped forward and pushed the door. It swung open. A light was still switched on inside, which surprised them: Aunt Edna was not the sort of aunt to leave a light on.

Inside the laboratory it looked as if a disastrous experiment had recently taken place. Broken test tubes and bottles glittered on the floor, mingling with damp pages of note books and files. The air smelled of dental surgeries and rotten eggs. Across the floor and out of the room shot three

white mice, a bright red snake and two black spiders the size of tennis-balls, each with a set of white, human teeth.

Aunty Anne went to a desk on which lay one of Aunt Edna's notebooks. Her radar eyes had spotted something *not quite right*.

In small, mean handwriting, the notebook listed all Aunt Edna's recent inventions, including electromagnetic school trousers and prefect badge bugging devices. The notebook had been left open on a page headed Bad Gas, but the part of the page below the heading had been carefully ripped out.

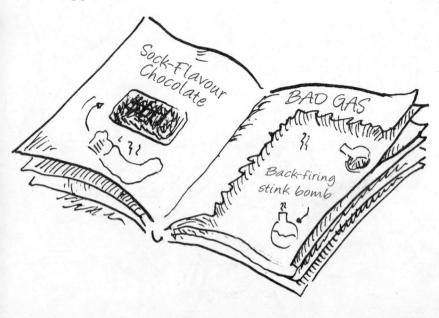

'Bad Gas!' said Aunty Anne. 'That's your Aunt Edna's secret formula for turning naughty children into maggots. If it's fallen into the wrong hands it could be disastrous. Come on Billy, Alfie. We've got to find out where your aunt is before her kidnappers learn how to make it.'

Billy and Alfie were glad to leave the uncomfortable cellar and return to the kitchen.

'It's very odd,' said Alfie to Aunty Anne as they sat eating their lunch of pizza and banoffi pie. 'You always know where Aunt Edna is. So why don't you know where she's disappeared to?'

'It baffles me,' admitted Aunty Anne.

'Who'd want to steal her anyway? They'd have to be complete weirdos!' said Billy. 'We would've given her away.'

'Weirdos…' Alfie murmured thoughtfully. 'Talking of weirdos, what about those weird men who tried to get you into their car, Aunty Anne? They tried to steal you, didn't they? What if they were really after Aunt Edna?'

'It must be them!' Billy said.

'Exactly. But the question is – where is she now?'

They began to wonder if they'd ever see their aunt again.

6

Day of the Giant Maggots

Billy and Alfie's first thought when they realized their aunt had gone was that they could eat pizza and chocolate cake every day and never go to school again.

'But what if something went wrong with Aunty Anne?'

'Yes, but—'

'And what about the Bad Gas? What if the men who stole her start turning all of us children into maggots?'

'Yes, but—'

'And also,' said Alfie, finally, 'I mean, Aunt Edna is a human being, isn't she? And our only relative …'

Billy didn't answer.

'It'd be wrong if we left her. If we did nothing, wouldn't it?'

'Would it?' asked Billy.

'I think so,' said Alfie philosophically.

'Then there's nothing for it,' Billy sighed. 'We'll just have to call the police.' He picked up his new mobile, pleased at least to have a reason to try it out.

'Wait a minute!' Alfie said. 'If we call the police, Aunty Anne would need to hide. If she hid then the police would send us back to the orphanage until they find her. And if they didn't find her we'd have to stay in the orphanage forever.'

'Oh,' said Billy, lowering his phone. 'Can't I call the police anyway?'

'No, Billy. We're just going to have to rescue Aunt Edna ourselves.'

'Can I use my telescopic catapult and new catapult?'

'We might need more than that,' murmured Alfie. 'But how are we going to find her?'

'Easy-queasy.' said Billy. 'Ask Aunty Anne tomorrow. Goodnight.'

Billy slept, but Alfie couldn't. She lay in the darkness, watching a cloud drift across the moon like a lost spacecraft. Why couldn't Aunty Anne tell where Aunt Edna was? Did it mean that Aunt Edna was…?

Suddenly Alfie felt very alone and very small in a big universe.

Early next morning they went down to breakfast to make a plan.

'If only we could remember the car number plate, maybe we could trace where it came from,' suggested Alfie.

'Remember the number plate! I can hardly remember the car!'

Suddenly Aunty Anne's eyes glowed a pale electric-lime colour, which illuminated the breakfast table and made the marmalade jar glitter. On the tablecloth a photo appeared of a black car with blacked-out windows.

'Where's that coming from?'

'A little video recorder just to the left of my right eye, Billy.'

'It's the car! And that's me!' It really was Billy, and he was just blocking the view of the number plate. Aunty Anne tried other views but somehow Billy was always in the way.

'Well, that's not much help,' concluded Aunty Anne.

But just at one point Billy skipped out of, then back into, the camera view. Aunty Anne replayed the sequence and froze the image.

'Brilliant!' said Alfie.

'Yes, brilliant!' said Billy. 'Um… What do we do with it?'

'We can trace the name of the driver through the car-register database.'

'What's that in English?'

'Look it up on the Internet.'

'Or ask me,' Aunty Anne interrupted politely. Her eyes glowed brightly: a square of white light flickered on the table-top, followed by a long list of numbers. One of the numbers was highlighted in blue.

'Cuthbert Sweetboy,' Billy read. 'You can't have a kidnapper called Cuthbert Sweetboy. That's a rubbish name. And anyway, even if he is the kidnapper, what's the point of knowing his name?'

'We need the criminal database for that,' said Alfie. 'But not even the Internet has that.'

'But I do,' said Aunty Anne. 'Now, let me see…' The white light flickered. The list was replaced with:

ULTRA-TOP SECRETS
For the eyes of the Prime Minister and MI6 only

Files

1. Most Dangerous Secret Weapons
2. UFO Sightings and captured Flying Saucers under investigation.
3. Most Dangerous International Criminals

'Ah, that looks hopeful,' Aunty Anne said and opened file 3.

International Criminals:
Most dangerous:

1. Cuthbert Sweetboy: for crimes against humanity, noses, and everything else.

'That's him!' said Alfie. 'And right at the very top of the list!'

'Isn't this illegal?' asked Billy excitedly and hopefully.

'Yes, isn't this what you'd call computer-hacking, Aunty Anne?' Alfie looked up at her.

'Well, not quite, Alfie,' Aunty Anne said. 'You see, I'm already a computer, so it's exactly like you asking a friend for some information. Also, you'll see your aunt is in the greatest possible danger if Cuthbert Sweetboy is the one who's kidnapped her.'

'Let's read what it says,' Billy said eagerly, pleased it was almost illegal.

'Cuthbert Sweetboy,' read Alfie, 'otherwise known, because of a facial defect, as "Nonose".'

'No nose? How does he smell? Terrible!' laughed Billy.

'Wait a minute,' Alfie said. 'No nose … That's him! The man who tried to drag Aunty Anne into the car. That's what was missing on his face.'

They read about the file information on Cuthbert Sweetboy.

History: Little is known of Nonose's life or how he lost his nose. Early school records show he had no friends, and worked hard in Chemistry, hoping to make a bomb to blow up the school. After completing his education he disappeared, but is now known to be linked to every major criminal organization throughout the world.

Ambitions: To take over the world and have everyone's noses removed.

Warning to all agents: This man is extremely dangerous. If contact is made ensure your nose is protected.

'Wow!' said Alfie, 'Aunt Edna is in danger.'
'Somehow,' said Aunty Anne, 'we've got to find where they've taken her.'

PROTECTIVE ANTI-NONOSE ARMOUR

SECURE TIGHTLY – IN CASE OF CONTACT, DO NOT REMOVE

'Can we see a picture of the car again?' asked Alfie. She'd noticed an orange sticker on the windscreen.

Aunty Anne quickly rewound the footage.

'Let's have a look.' Her eyes gave a low hum and the orange sticker on the windscreen filled the table-top.

'It's advertising the garage where they bought the car,' Alfie read. 'I can just make out "Wiltshire". Somewhere in Wiltshire.'

'Wiltshire. Well,' said Billy, 'That's really helpful. Only the whole of Wiltshire to search. That's all. Shouldn't take more than a couple of years.'

'Now, now, Billy,' said Aunty Anne. 'We'll think of something.'

'Can't we just leave Aunt Edna where she is?' Billy asked.

The ultra-violet rays lit up Aunt Edna's note book. 'There are molecules of Bad Gas on this page,' Aunty Anne said. 'If we get close enough, I'll be able to smell the gas on the torn piece of paper the kidnappers have taken.'

'That's called "forensics",' Alfie said. 'Isn't it, Aunty Anne?'

'It's called flipping brilliant!' Billy said. 'But we've got to get close enough.'

'For that we'll need a car.'

Mr Snugbug hadn't seen Aunt Edna for three days and was taking it out on Justin. He'd been sent to bed early twice and on Thursday night his burgers had been burnt into dry, black, flying saucers. Both were relieved when at eight o'clock that Friday morning Billy and Alfie and Aunty Anne stepped out of 59 Screw Drive and joined them in their usual walk to school.

'We've been very worried about you, haven't we, Justin?' Mr Snugbug said.

'Haven't stopped thinking about you,' Justin mumbled. It was true that Justin and his dad had, in their different ways, been thinking deeply about their neighbours.

'It's half term next week, Edna,' Mr Snugbug said as they reached the school gate. 'Justin and I are thinking of a camping holiday. Aren't we, Justin?'

'Are we?' Justin seemed surprised and more than a little appalled. He couldn't think of anything worse. When they went on holiday they always stayed at the poshest hotels.

'Perhaps you'd like to join us. Go into the countryside. Take the car.'

'Car?' said Billy.

'Countryside?' said Alfie.

'Wiltshire?' suggested Aunty Anne.

'Wiltshire? That's a good idea, isn't it, Justin?'

'Is it?'

'We've always been meaning to go to Wiltshire, haven't we, Justin?' Mr Snugbug beamed.

'Have we?' Justin scowled.

And so it was agreed. They would leave the next day.

* * *

Aunt Edna sat in the children's bedroom gazing at the bare grey walls and bare floorboards. Except it wasn't their bedroom. It was an attic room in an isolated farmhouse somewhere in Wiltshire. And the door was solid steel with four locks. As she contemplated one of the walls, she heard, one by one, each of the locks being opened. She had heard these sounds at exactly the same time each morning for a week.

As usual, a wide, unusually squat man entered with her breakfast.

'Mmm,' the man said, 'I wonder what delicious meal

'as been prepared for you this sunny morning. Is it scrambled eggs with smoked salmon? No. Is it waffles with maple syrup and fresh runny cream? No. Let's 'ave a look, shall we? Oh, it's your lucky day! It's bread and water again!'

The man entertained Aunt Edna with this little speech every morning and every morning served the plate of ancient bread and glass of stale water.

'I don't expect you're enjoying living in this horrible room, are you?' The man turned his metal funnel ear towards Aunt Edna.

Aunt Edna looked about her. 'Why would that bother me?'

'Well, I don't expect you want to have to eat

bread and drink water again, do you?'

'Why would that bother me?'

'Well, I don't expect you like sitting here all day without any computer games to play, or Sudoku problems, not even a TV to watch, do you?'

'Why would that bother me?'

The kidnappers did not seem to know how to make Aunt Edna's life any worse. In fact, it was no worse than at 59 Screw Drive. Aunt Edna sat quite contentedly all day thinking up new inventions and storing them in her head. The only difference was that if the kidnappers succeeded in forcing her inventions out of her, it would be a short step to them taking over the world.

As Aunt Edna's fourth day of captivity began, back at number 59, Alfie and Billy were packing. Alfie and Billy didn't know Justin had already filled the boot with large quantities of Porky's Perfect Pizzas. Justin didn't know that Billy and Alfie's suitcases were crammed with Bob's Bigger Burgers and Cheeki Choko Cherry Cakes.

The morning was spangled with sunlight, the air as clear as a cow-bell tinkle. This was fortunate as it meant that, as they reached Wiltshire, Aunty Anne's electronic nose quickly picked up the dangerous molecules of Bad Gas.

'At the roundabout take the second exit,' Aunty Anne announced. 'Continue five hundred metres, then turn left at the junction by the Old Organic Farm Shop.'

'How do you know all this?' marvelled Mr Snugbug. 'You sound like my old Sat Nav!'

It was Mr Snugbug's old Sat Nav. Aunt Edna had found it in his bin.

By mid-afternoon they reached the farmhouse where Aunt Edna was imprisoned. Bordering the fields surrounding the farmhouse was a stretch of woodland which made the perfect place to keep watch on the house.

'Let's strike camp here,' suggested Aunty Anne very firmly, and Mr Snugbug obediently parked the car behind the bushes.

Justin, who had demanded the most expensive and comfortable tent in the shop, left his dad to pitch it.

'Now just watch what I do, Edna,' Mr Snugbug insisted. 'Then I'll help you with yours.'

Billy and Alfie sat and watched as Mr Snugbug gradually embedded himself in a cocoon of heavy canvas, whilst Justin got more and more enraged to see the other tent raised in minutes by Aunty Anne.

'Need any help, Mr Snugbug?' asked Billy.

'No, no! Nearly done!' a muffled voice called out in the twilight.

It was also Mr Snugbug who insisted they make a real fire to cook on.

'I was in the Boy Scouts,' he boasted.

When all the matches in the box had been used up and the gas in the lighter all burnt and darkness seeped down from the trees, Mr Snugbug suggested a cold buffet.

'Aunty Anne,' Billy whispered, 'light the fire.'

'Let me try, Mr Snug— Morris.'

In the darkness, only Alfie and Billy saw the glow from Aunty Anne's eyes igniting the pieces of wood.

'Wow!' whispered Billy, 'Laser eyes!'

'Aunt Edna was in the Girl Guides,' Alfie explained quickly.

Justin was anxious not to have to share his supply of Porky's Perfect Pizzas. When he saw the variety of Bob's Bigger Burgers appearing in the firelight, however, he felt perhaps it might not be so harmful to show a little generosity.

Billy and Alfie had been keen to keep their Bob's Bigger Burgers to themselves, but when they saw Porky's Perfect Pizzas piled up in the boot, they felt it would do no harm to show a little generosity.

'Justin, you must try one of our burgers,' said Billy, as the smell of roasting beef filled the night.

'Go nicely with a slice of pizza, I expect,' Justin managed. And then, with the greatest difficulty, 'Wan' a bit?'

* * *

Aunty Anne's eyes glowed red in the dark as she
sat on her portable recharger.

'If we can't find Aunt Edna or rescue her,' Billy
said, sitting on his sleeping bag, 'Mr Snugbug
could marry Aunty Anne. Then, if she ever went
wrong, he would still be our dad and have to look
after us.'

'We've been through this already. Mr Snugbug
would know the difference in the end,' said Alfie,
who'd read a lot about how grown-ups lived and
what they got up to when they were married.

'I don't know why they've kidnapped Aunt
Edna anyway. I mean, they've got the Bad Gas
formula, but why do they want to turn naughty

children into giant maggots?'

Aunty Anne's eyes turned green; her batteries were charged. 'There's a very good reason, Billy,' she said. 'The formula could be adjusted, then it could turn good grown-ups into maggots instead. Like policemen. Or teachers.'

'Some teachers already are maggots,' Billy said.

'And then, if they were all maggots, we'd have no one to stop the kidnappers doing what they wanted.'

'Wouldn't be such a bad life being a maggot. They spend all day eating.'

'Yes, but look what they eat. Besides, they turn into flies in the end.'

'Even better! We could fly!'

'Yes, until you're swatted,' said Alfie.

The children remained silent for a moment. 'If we save Aunt Edna and Mr Snugbug marries her,' Billy said, 'you would still look after us, wouldn't you?'

'Even I don't know that, Billy,' said Aunty Anne. 'And something else I don't know is why I'm convinced your aunt is in the house, although I can't sense her presence. The Bad Gas smell is so strong.'

Again, Alfie felt uneasy. Surely, she thought, it really can mean only one thing…

Flying to the Moon

In the most comfortable room in the farmhouse sat the most evil man in the world.

That spring morning he'd been woken from a dream of Father Christmas by two wood pigeons cooing in a tree just under his bedroom window. Although he was now about to eat one of them with his toast and marmalade, it didn't cheer him up. The delicious smell of roast pigeon filled the room from the kitchen, but the man couldn't smell it as he didn't have a nose.

'And you've kept Professor Stepford in that room the whole time?' he was saying.

'She don't mind the room, boss,' said the man with the funnel ear, as he placed the cooked pigeon, rack of toast and pot of marmalade on

the white tablecloth.

'And you've given her only bread and water?'

'She don't mind bread and water, boss.'

'And she's got no TV?'

'She don't mind no TV, boss.'

'No TV? But human beings can't cope without TVs.'

'But you do and you're a human being … aren't you, boss?'

'I am a special human being, Tinear.'

'Yes, boss.'

'There must be something she wants. Everyone wants something.'

'Yes, boss.'

'And I want that second pigeon now. Is it ready?'

'Yes, boss.'

'Well, don't just stand there, Tinear. Are you deaf?'

'Well, now you mention it, boss, this tin-ear of mine—'

'Go and get it!

'Yes, boss.'

Aunt Edna had everything she wanted, or nothing more than she had when she was at 59 Screw Drive. She had never understood why people needed any comfort. Holidays were a mystery to her: what was the point of going somewhere hot and sitting on a beach? Some people, she thought, even liked camping! However, as she sat there working on a dress-up-doll computer game, she suddenly felt an urge for a Cheeki Choko Cherry Cake.

'Rubbish!' she thought to herself. 'I don't need a Choko Cake. I can do quite well without one. Nevertheless, it would've been, well … nice, just about this time of the morning … to help with the concentration.' Aunt Edna tried to stop herself thinking about it, but the chocolate-dripping biscuit, layered with thin spreads of cherry jam and vanilla cream kept reappearing in her mind.

* * *

Before they went on their walk that morning, the camping party shared a pot of tea and a plate of Cheeki Choko Cherry Cakes. The cakes were the last of the charity race prize, but since he was allowed to share them, Justin had forgiven Billy and Alfie for robbing him of them.

Mr Snugbug had suggested the walk, believing it would be romantic to stroll through the bluebell woods with Aunt Edna. Billy and Alfie thought it would be good because Aunty Anne could spy on the farmhouse. Justin thought it would be good to shoot at things with his new catapult.

Mr Snugbug
and Aunty Anne
strolled ahead through
a cathedral of pink and
lilac blossom. They
heard the gurgle of an
invisible stream, the
tunes of twelve different
birds, and the *thwack,
thwack, thwack!* percussion
of Justin's catapult.

'We've got to separate
Mr Snugbug from Aunty
Anne,' Billy whispered to
Alfie. 'She can't use her

X-ray eyes with Snugbug staring into them the whole time.'

Alfie, as always, had an idea. She approached Justin's dad.

'Mr Snugbug,' she drew him away from the others. 'Did you know Aunt Edna is a great bird watcher? Well, up in that tree there I noticed her favourite – the lesser-speckled black-tit. If you could get some film of *that*, she'd *love* it.'

Mr Snugbug, naturally afraid of heights, gazed up at the upper branches of the tall trunk. After only a moment's hesitation, however, he strapped his camcorder onto his back and started to climb. When he was half-way up, Aunty Anne turned towards the farmhouse. Her eyes began

to glow. She gazed for a long time. But the X-ray
eyes failed to penetrate the wall.

'We need to get closer,' she said.

'We can't do that. They might see us.'

'I've got it!' said Billy. 'Aunty Anne, turn
yourself into a cow.'

'Don't be stupid,' Alfie said.

'Even I can't do that, Billy. But I can do this.'

She looked back at the house. Suddenly her
eyes began to bulge and the next moment, her
eyeballs sprang out and flew across the field,

attached to thin red electric
flex. About mid-field they
stopped and hovered.

'Blimey!' said Alfie.

'Wow!' said Billy.

'Now that's what
I call being "long-
sighted".'

'Is she there, Aunty Anne?'

'I'm afraid I can't tell. But at least I know why I can't see through the walls. They've been lined with lead. They must've read about your aunt's tracking device in the notebook. That's why I can't locate her.'

This was good news to Alfie. It meant that Aunt Edna could be alive, and even kicking, after all!

Suddenly from the wood came a distressed yelp. Aunty Anne's eyeballs shot back into place, like pool balls into their pockets.

Back in the woods, they found Mr Snugbug straddled across the branch of a tree on his stomach. His feet and arms dangled on either side. A couple of lesser-speckled black-tits, or whatever birds they really were, dive-bombed Mr Snugbug, making him yelp even more.

'Oh, no! We've got to help him,' Alfie said.

'Easy-queasy,' said Aunty Anne. With spider-speed, she scuttled up the tree trunk and was soon helping Mr Snugbug back along the branch. It was just then that Justin turned his catapult on one of the lesser-speckled black-tits.

'This'll teach those birds a lesson,' he said.

Before Billy or Alfie could stop him, he fired.

Thwack!

The first pellet bounced harmlessly off Aunty Anne's head. Justin fired another. The second pellet bounced off her eyeball. He fired two more with similar results. By this time Mr Snugbug had reached the lower branches and jumped safely onto the ground.

'This catapult's useless!' Justin said. 'The pellets don't do anything. Look!'

He shot his dad in the foot.

'Aargh!' said Mr Snugbug. The pellet had hit

the bruise left when Justin had stamped on his foot in the sports day race.

'You … you … evil boy!' he screamed.

'Oops,' said Justin, and then looked with renewed suspicion at Aunty Anne.

* * *

'Forty-five millimetres of solid steel and lined with lead,' said Aunty Anne that night in the tent. Billy and Alfie were preparing a midnight snack. They'd poured corn into a pot and milk and cocoa powder into cups. Aunty Anne's laser-eyes focused on the pot until the corn began exploding. Then she looked at the cups and steam rose from the cocoa.

'But can't you burn though the walls with your lasers?'

'The window-shutters are reinforced steel. They might take less time, but only by about 75 minutes and 35 seconds.'

'Oh. That's a real problem with Snugbug and Justin around all the time.' The corn had stopped popping. Billy lifted the lid and stuffed some hot popcorn into his mouth. 'Justin's getting very suspicious of you.'

'Yes,' agreed Alfie. 'I'm sure he saw the

pellet bounce off your eyeball.'

'I certainly saw it!' said Aunty Anne.

'Aunty Anne!' laughed Alfie. 'You told a joke!'

'So I did!'

'But I'm sure Justin saw it too,' Billy said.

'I *thought* so,' said a voice from outside the tent. A head popped through the flap.

'Justin!' Billy gulped.

'Popcorn!' Justin said. 'I could smell it a mile away.'

Alfie, quickly recovering from the shock, stepped out of the tent with the pot of popcorn. 'Glad you could join us, Justin. Here, help yourself.'

Then Billy and Aunty Anne came out too and found Mr Snugbug a few metres away staring romantically up at the moon. 'Ah, Edna! Just look at that full moon.' He stepped closer to her. 'It looks almost near enough to touch, doesn't it?'

'I don't think so, Mr Snug— Morris. It's 384,400 kilometres away.'

'Well, yes, but…'

Justin burped loudly. With the popcorn finished, he demanded to return immediately to their tent. Mr Snugbug sighed, and reluctantly wished everyone goodnight.

'Phew!' said Billy. 'That was close. How on

earth are we going to rescue Aunt Edna without them knowing? What's more, what will happen if they see Aunt Edna and Aunty Anne together?'

It was this last thought that made Alfie think of the Perfect Plan to rescue Aunt Edna.

'Actually,' said Billy, 'Mr Snugbug's right. It does look like you can touch the moon…'

Suddenly, without saying anything, Aunty Anne's arms circled the children's waists. Billy and Alfie rose up into the night sky and they felt the stars around them.

They felt the
coolness of the
evening air, and down
below, a long, long way
away, in a meadow they
couldn't see, they heard
a single lamb bleating.
For a while they lingered
in midair, until Aunty
Anne's legs retracted and
down they came.

'Wow!' said Billy
and Alfie together.

'Time for bed,'
said Aunty Anne.

* * *

That night, while Alfie dreamed up the Perfect Plan, Aunt Edna dreamed violently of Cheeki Choko Cherry Cakes.

When Tinear entered her room in the morning with her bread and water, she felt for the first time that there might be more to life than work.

Choko Cakes.

Her mind had become obsessed with getting one. She thought she'd have to try being nice to Tinear, which was difficult, as she'd never been nice to anyone.

'Why are you so ugly?' she began.

Tinear glared at her, stunned.

'Why have you got a fat metal thumb?'

Tinear's expression grew more stern.

'Why have you got a metal eyelid?'

Tinear's face turned red with anger and the metal eyelid twitched.

'Why have you got a funnel for an ear?' Aunt Edna continued. 'You ought to get that fixed.'

For a moment Tinear looked as if he might well fix Aunt Edna's face.

'IT 'AS BEEN FIXED!' he exploded. The

funnel ear flew out. He picked it up and jammed it back into his head. 'Cost me a fortune, it did.'

'But I'm a scientist,' said Aunt Edna, 'I could mend your whole face properly.'

'Properly?'

'Yes. So it looked normal.'

Tinear sat down. 'Normal?' He paused. 'Don't it look normal then?'

He took a wallet from his pocket and produced a photo. It was Tinear when he didn't have a tin ear. Or a metal eyelid. Or a metal thumb. 'That was before,' he said. 'Before the boss promised to give me all this money if I put a bomb in a bank one night. I forgot when it was timed to go off. I 'ad to use the money he gave me to get fixed up.' He looked at the photo. 'Can you make me look like this again?'

'Better.'

'Better!' The metal eyelid squeaked open suspiciously. 'Better? Why would I want to look better than that? I was 'andsome.'

'All right, then. Just as good.'

'And what do you want?'

Aunt Edna paused, then said, 'You don't happen to have a Cheeki Choko Cherry Cake in the kitchen, do you?'

8

The Perfect Plan

Mr Snugbug couldn't believe his luck. He'd tried everything to make Aunt Edna think he was a fantastic human being, without success, and now, here he was, being offered the hero's role in *Escape from Hellfire Farm*, the Stepford family's action-packed movie!

It had happened after lunch, the day after their walk. Alfie had shown Mr Snugbug and Justin a film-script she'd written. It was an exciting story about the kidnapping of Zoe Faircheek by evil criminals, one without a nose and one with a tin ear. The two villains were holding Zoe prisoner in an empty farmhouse. Special Agent Mike Strength manages to find the farmhouse and, with the help of his young partner, Alex Triggerfinger

– the crack-shot with a catapult – engineer a daring rescue.

'We want you, Mr Snugbug, to play Mike Strength,' Billy said. 'We think you'd be exactly right for the part, don't we, Alfie?'

'What's Mike Strength like?' asked Mr Snugbug.

'He's brilliantly clever,' read Alfie. 'Athletic, handsome and brave. You'd be perfect, Mr Snugbug. Wouldn't he, Aunt Edna?'

'I can't think of anyone more fitting that description,' Aunty Anne answered as instructed.

'But what about Alex Triggerfinger?' Justin asked, angry he wasn't to be included.

'Any ideas, anyone?' Billy gazed about him slyly.

'Well, what about me?' Justin cried out.

'Gosh!' said Billy. 'You'd be perfect! Why didn't I think of it before!'

Justin's face brightened, and he ran off to fetch his catapult.

'And Zoe Faircheek?' asked Mr Snugbug tentatively.

'Aunt Edna, of course,' said Billy.

* * *

It seemed to Aunt Edna that this was the best Cheeki Choko Cherry Cake she'd ever tasted. Chocolate, cherry, cream and sugar flooded her whole body and mind with well-being. But it also filled it with a vague sense of guilt. Sitting in the hard wooden chair in the bare room, she began to look about her and see how uncomfortable her life had been since she got here.

This got her thinking how uncomfortable her life had been for … well … for about twenty years. And for the first time ever, she began to think how miserable it must be for Billy and Alfie, too.

She took another Choko Cake from the plate Tinear had left her for breakfast. Perhaps, her thoughts continued, the Masterchef Machine recipes could be altered to give them a taste of a Cheeki Choko Cherry Cake once in a while…

The mouth-watering smell of charcoal-grilled burger and sausage weaved about the campsite as the Stepfords and Snugbugs gathered round for their barbecue lunch. The morning had been spent in rehearsals for *Escape from Hellfire Farm* and now they were all very hungry.

'This afternoon we'll do the big escape scene,' said Alfie, biting into a hotdog. 'Have you checked the car, Mr Snugbug? We don't want to have to reshoot, after all.'

'All systems go!' said Mr Snugbug, no longer Mr Snugbug nor Justin's dad, but Mike Strength, Special Agent.

'And Justin. Your catapult's ready for action?'

Justin raised his catapult from where it sat at his side and dipped his sausage into a cow pat-sized mound of tomato sauce.

By the time they'd finished eating, the sun was poised above the tree-tops. Aunty Anne offered round the very last Cheeki Choko Cherry Cakes. No one wanted one. They were sick to death of Choko Cakes.

'Action!' said Billy, and they began filming the first scenes of *Escape from Hellfire Farm*.

It wasn't always easy to guess what Nonose was thinking, but it was safe to say it was always bad. As he stared out through the thin slit of the window-shutter, he wasn't thinking of the shimmering

light on the golden fields surrounding
him, the greens and violet shadows
of the woodlands beyond, the faint
veil of smoke riding across the
treetops, but of all the people he'd
turn into giant maggots.

There was Russell Knucklebutt,
who'd bullied him at school
in Year 3, for instance. Mr
Spikebonce, the gym teacher.
Superintendent Oakarm
of Special Branch, and

Percival, his brother, the
well-known children's
book illustrator.
Then he
opened up a
little lacquer
box on the table
and saw inside the curl of soft
golden wool. And this led him to
think of Uncle Alphonse and the Terrible Event
that made his nose disappear. When he was little,

Nonose – or Cuthbert as he was then – was never without Rosebud, his teddy. Until one day Uncle Alphonse, on a visit, said that he was too old to have a teddy. He grabbed the bear from Cuthbert's arms and threw it on the garden bonfire, where it flared up with the burning wood.

Cuthbert watched with disbelief as Rosebud began to burn. He was so horror-struck, he dived into the fire too. Yet, before he could rescue his most treasured friend, Uncle Alphonse had grabbed his foot and pulled Cuthbert away from the flames.

In that moment, Cuthbert lost both Rosebud and his nose – burnt to a snotty crisp. It left him in a world in which he wanted to destroy everything – especially nice people and their noses.

After this Nonose never smiled or cried again. In fact, his face hardly moved again – and nor did his thoughts. The thoughts became simpler and simpler: destroy the world, destroy the universe, kick Tinear.

If Uncle Alphonse had still been alive, Nonose would have used him as a guinea-pig for the Bad Gas formula, but now Nonose needed someone else. He was trying to think who to choose when Tinear knocked on the door.

'Enter!' Nonose called in his high-pitched voice. 'Ah! Just the person I was thinking of. Well? Any change?'

'No, boss.'

'She still doesn't mind living in that room?'

'No, boss.'

'And she still doesn't mind not having a TV?'

'No, boss.'

'And she still doesn't mind eating and drinking

only bread and water?'

'N-no, boss,' said Tinear, his metal eyelid twitching and squeaking nervously with the lie.

Nonose turned from the window. 'If something doesn't happen soon, Tinear, I will have to make it happen.'

Whenever Nonose made something happen, it was usually painful, and Tinear was usually the one who felt it.

'Y-yes, boss.'

But just then, something did happen. When Nonose turned back to the window he noticed a movement from the shadow of the woods, just below where the coil of smoke rose.

Something was approaching very fast across the track between the fields. A car. It looked as if it was heading straight towards the farmhouse. In fact, it *was* heading straight towards the house.

It swerved to a halt just in front of the window. While the driver revved the engine, a boy in the back seat fired a catapult wildly at Nonose. The next moment, Professor Stepford jumped down from the roof of the farmhouse, ran to the car and leapt in.

'Tinear, you tin-head, you've let her escape!' Nonose screeched.

'But – but – boss, she can't have. She's locked up. I locked all four locks. I always lock all four locks. That's what I always do.'

'Who do you think you just saw then, tin for brains, her double?'

'No, boss.'

'Well, don't just stand there. Get the car!'

Tinear hurried out while Nonose watched the escaping vehicle bumping across the fields along with his dreams of world power.

Moments later, Tinear appeared in the familiar long black car with the blacked-out windows. Nonose leapt into the passenger seat and the car roared off in pursuit.

* * *

Silence surrounded the house, except for the chirping from the nest disturbed when Aunty Anne had stood on the window-ledge above. Her telescopic legs had taken her there.

'The door's open.' Billy pushed it and they stepped into the equally silent, cool hallway. Nonose and Tinear were gone.

Billy and Alfie were pleased that Aunty Anne was back with them. She'd leapt out of the car while Nonose and Tinear were distracted, telling Mr Snugbug she was going to help Billy and Alfie

film the getaway.

'Well?' Alfie turned anxiously to Aunty Anne. 'Can you sense Aunt Edna now?'

'No,' she said, confused for the first time in her electronic life. 'No, I can't.'

'I know she's here,' said Alfie warmly, 'I can feel it.'

'But where, exactly?' Billy said, eager to get out as soon as possible.

'She must be upstairs,' Aunty Anne said, 'I can see into the rooms downstairs, but not the two rooms upstairs.'

'Let's go!'

Billy leapt up the staircase. He'd just got to the top, when Aunty Anne reached out to stop him with a telescopic arm.

'There's someone in the corridor,' she whispered as she joined him. They listened, holding their breath, except Aunty Anne, who didn't breathe, of course.

'They might have a weapon,' whispered Alfie.

Aunty Anne moved closer to the wall, and then her eyeballs popped out, attached to the thin cables, and slithered like snakes across the carpet. They peeped round the corner.

'They haven't *got* a weapon,' she said. 'They *are* a weapon!'

As her eyes sprang back into place, they heard

someone – or rather something – making its way up the corridor, dragging itself across the carpet, something very heavy and … moist. A huge great maggot appeared round the corner, filling the landing like a tube train in a tunnel. It screamed with a thin, high-pitched note, revealing sharp little rows of pink teeth.

'Blast it with your lasers, Aunty Anne!'

'I can't. They've adapted the Bad Gas formula! That maggot's a good person.'

'Doesn't look as if it's going to be good to us.' Billy stepped back.

'It's going to eat us alive!' said Alfie.

The maggot had cornered them.

The next second, Alfie and Billy felt themselves lifted over its head and dangling above the huge, pink hole of its mouth. Then they were falling to the floor just behind the maggot's tail.

'Aunty Anne to the rescue again!' said Alfie, as Aunty Anne's telescopic legs retracted.

The maggot struggled and squirmed, trying to turn round in the narrow corridor. As it did, it stretched its neck and nipped Aunty Anne's foot. If it had been a human foot the foot would no longer be there. When the maggot's teeth gripped Aunty Anne, however, they bent like rubber and it immediately screamed and let go.

'That's what I call "giving it the boot"!' said Billy as they hurried to the upstairs rooms.

'But isn't it too late?' said Alfie. 'This means they already have the formula.'

'We've still got to rescue Aunt Edna,' said Billy, 'She is our only relative, after all.'

Upstairs, there were two rooms. The door of the room on the right was already open, and was

empty. The door on the left was locked – four times.

'Four locks!' said Alfie. 'We'll never open those.'

'Aunty Anne, you can blast them with your lasers.'

'Not those, Billy. Nor the door. They're solid steel. It would take 37 minutes and 30 seconds and we don't have that long. We must find the keys. They wouldn't have taken them: the keys must be enormous.'

'If they're that big, Aunty Anne, you can find them.'

The green rays illuminated the corridor and then the carpet as she scanned the floor below.

'Nothing,' she said.

'Nothing?' Alfie was

surprised. 'But they must be here somewhere.'

'If Aunty Anne can't find them, it means the keys aren't here.'

'No keys?' Alfie said, and looked at the locks again. She noticed they protruded unusually from the door.

'There's something funny about these locks,' she said. 'Not the usual double-lock pin-tumblers.'

'Double-lock bin-crumblers? How do you know what they are?'

'Well, I—'

'Don't tell me. You read it in a book.'

Alfie knelt down and examined the locks. She looked through the keyhole but saw only blackness: the hole seemed to be blocked. Then she noticed the grip-lines around the perimeter of the lock.

As she gripped, the lock turned like a switch! Three locks later, the door swung open...

* * *

'That's odd,' said Mr Snugbug. 'There really is a car chasing us! It's just like … for real!'

Mr Snugbug was driving fast down the country road. He really did believe now he *was* Mike Strength so had completely forgotten he was out of camera-shot.

'Shall I fire at them?' suggested Justin. 'Yes, I'll shoot at them. That'll be even more realistic!'

'Boss,' said Tinear. 'They're shooting at us.'

'Well, shoot back at them! Kill them all!'

'I left my gun in the 'ouse.'

'You tin-turd. If you don't kill them I'll kill you! Personally.'

Thinking how Professor Stepford promised to fix his face and how killing her would make this promise difficult for her to keep, Tinear decided – for the first time in his life – to put his foot down. On the brake pedal.

'What're you doing, you tin twit!' said Nonose as the car screeched to a halt.

In reply Tinear smashed his fist right into the centre of Nonose's face.

Very slowly, a lump rose just where his nose should have been.

'There you are, boss,' said Tinear to the unconscious Nonose, 'a new nose without surgery. An' I ain't even goin' to charge you.'

He felt unexpectedly pleased with himself.

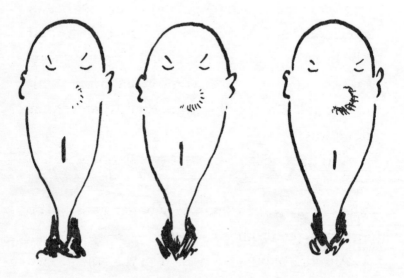

'They've stopped. Perhaps I've killed them,' said Justin, just a tiny bit worried.

Mr Snugbug stopped too. 'That was exciting,' said Mr Snugbug. 'I hope Billy got it all on film.'

Aunt Edna had long since finished all the Cheeki Choko Cherry Cakes and was beginning to want some more. She wanted other things too. Perhaps it would be nice to go for a walk in the park. Or see what state the sky was in that morning. Or gaze for a while at a buttercup. And again she began to feel some guilt about how she'd made Alfie and Billy live like children in some sad Victorian story. She sat there for a long time wondering about her life and Billy and his little sister (whatever her name was…).

And then her prison door swung open.

Alfie's heart leapt when she saw her aunt in the corner of the room.

'Alfreda! Billy!' she cried. 'You've come to save me! You've given me a second chance. Another chance to become a real aunt! I've been sitting here thinking all about it, about how I haven't cared for you. It's been going round and round in my brain like a maths problem.

'The first thing I'll do is convert the Masterchef Machine to make pizzas and burgers. You'll like that, won't you? And we'll get rid of that mechanical monster I made to look after you...'

Billy and Alfie turned to Aunty Anne in dismay, but she was already out of the house and sprinting across the fields back to 59 Screw Drive.

'Aunt Edna's cracked,'

whispered Billy to Alfie, as they helped her to her feet.

'I don't know if she's cracked or more sane,' Alfie said. 'But let's get out of here quickly.'

Taking hold of a hand each, they directed their aunt towards the door. Once on the landing, they hurried to the stairs, and then suddenly saw what was waiting for them on the floor below. It was worse than a giant maggot – it was *three* giant maggots. They hissed their high-pitched screams, sticky juices oozing from their skin as they slithered towards them.

'This is terrible!' Billy said. Then they heard a hiss behind them: the first maggot had woken up. 'Worse than terrible! We're surrounded. We're dead meat.'

'They like that best,' Alfie said. 'I read—'

'Don't worry,' Aunt Edna suddenly said, as the beasts approached. 'It's almost time.'

'Time?'

'Yes, they must've turned them into maggots about ten minutes ago. I heard Tinear open the door of their room. The formula only works for

ten minutes – I wouldn't tell them how to make it last longer. That's the information they needed. Well, it's nearly ten minutes.'

The maggots closed in on them. Needle-sharp teeth loomed and dripped above them, and they could smell the monsters' breath – a sickly-sweet smell of rotting flesh.

Suddenly, the maggots stopped screaming, wobbled like jellies, and shrank into a family of four. 'What are you doing in our house?' said the woman.

'Your house?'

'Yes,' said the man. 'This is our house. It's our farm.'

'We've been locked in our bedroom for days,' said the daughter.

The son added, 'All we've had to eat is—'

'Bread and water,' Aunt Edna said.

'How do you know that?'

Before Aunt Edna could reply, Billy cried, 'Come on!' and taking her hand pulled her towards the open door. Waiting outside was Mr Snugbug's car. So surprised by this, Aunt Edna allowed herself to be directed into the back seat by Justin Snugbug, who prodded her amicably enough with his catapult. She sat between Billy and Alfie and, after her astonishment had subsided, felt curiously full of an unfamiliar warmth for Billy and Alfie ... and even for Mr Snugbug ... Morris.

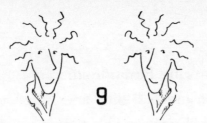

9

The Return of the Aunts

Anyone looking at the occupants of the car as they drove home would have thought they were looking at one big happy family. And Billy and Alfie were happy except for one thing. If Aunt Edna really had become the loving, caring person she promised to be – what would become of Aunty Anne? They were soon to find out.

Just before reaching Screw Drive, Mr Snugbug turned into the supermarket car park. 'Wait a moment, I've a few things to buy…' he said, smiling in a meaningful way at Aunt Edna.

When he and Justin had gone, Aunt Edna turned to Alfie and Billy and said, 'While we've been driving, I've been thinking how I can turn the catapult bed into a wide-screen television for you.

Then there's just the android…'

Just the android! Billy and Alfie looked wide-eyed at each other. The Snugbugs returned at that moment with four plump carrier bags which they put in the boot.

'Amazing,' said Mr Snugbug. 'Just saw the headlines of the *Bretford Express*. They've caught the most wanted criminal alive, and guess where? A mile from the very place where we were filming! Unbelievable! There we were acting out a dangerous mission when there were really dangerous criminals around the corner! And we didn't even know it!' He laughed.

59 Screw Drive looked very much the same. Mr Snugbug deposited their luggage, along with the carrier bags on the doorstep. 'Some supplies so you can enjoy a really tasty supper,' he said with a wink. 'After all, Edna, I know exactly what you like!' he announced.

'Oh, how thoughtful of you, Mr Snugbug.'

'Morris, please…'

'Morris. In fact, why don't you and Justin come for dinner too?'

'I was hoping you'd say that. Yes, we'd be delighted.'

It was just as Aunt Edna turned the lock of the front door that Alfie and Billy realized they'd forgotten to ask Aunty Anne to clear up the mess as soon as she got back. When Aunt Edna entered the front room she tripped on four empty burger boxes, and landed in the remains of a four-cheese pizza.

Standing up she saw takeaway cartons and DVD boxes lying like playing-cards all over the living room carpet. In the kitchen the draining board, table, even the floor, were stacked with plates and dishes covered with decaying food. The sink buzzed with over-excited flies.

Aunt Edna kicked an empty lemonade bottle across the linoleum. It rolled under a chair on which sat Aunty Anne, her eyes glowing red as she recharged herself.

'All this mess … and all this rubbishy food you've been eating,' Aunt Edna said. 'We're very fortunate that kind Mr Snugbug – Morris – has given us some nutritious supplies.'

Opening the bags she found only more burger boxes, frozen pizzas, microwave chips and a mountain of ice-cream and cake. Just then the phone rang.

'Yes?' Aunt Edna said sharply. 'Oh, it's you, is it? What do you think you're playing at with all this junk food? You wonder what time to come round, Mr Snugbug? I don't think so! There's no supper for you here tonight – nor for Billy or Alfrieda. They'll be going straight to bed!'

The next morning Billy and Alfie were flipped out of their catapult beds and served their Masterchef sausages, as usual.

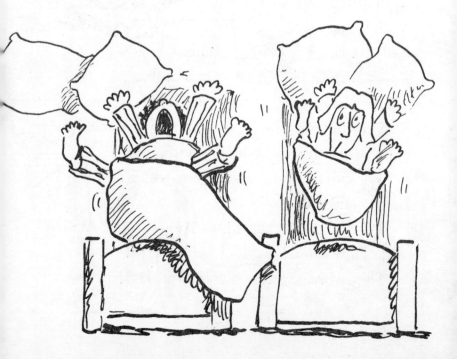

'At least things are back to normal,' said Alfie.

'And Aunty Anne is safe,' said Billy.

'I've really missed her, yet she was only with us yesterday.'

'Seems ages.'

As soon as they were out of the house with Aunty Anne, marching to school at the usual pace, Billy stamped on her foot.

Nothing happened.

'It's not working!' Billy said in panic. He tried again. Aunty Anne marched on. 'She's broken.'

'No, she's somehow fixed,' said Alfie in despair.

The thought that Aunty Anne was gone for good struck them with horror and misery.

'We can't live in that house without Aunty Anne,' said Billy

'We can't live at all without Aunty Anne,' Alfie said. 'How can we ever get her back?'

They worried about it all day at school.

On the way home, just before they entered Screw Drive, they had one final go at stamping on her foot.

It was difficult to tread on her feet when she was moving so fast and Billy's well-aimed foot missed entirely.

'Ow!' he yelped.

They didn't have much time. As Alfie made her last attempt, her foot slipped slightly and landed squarely on Aunty Anne's little toe.

For a moment, nothing happened.

Then her eyelids blinked and the rubber and plastic muscles under Aunty Anne's face transformed her mouth into that familiar smile.

'Ah, there you are,' she said, as if she'd been asleep. I *thought* I'd felt something when that maggot bit me. Even androids should be careful around dangerous animals.'

'Hurrah!' said Billy. 'Now we'll have the Saturday shop again and our finances will be back in order!'

'It's better than that,' said Alfie. 'We've got our aunt back in order.'

Alfie took hold of one of Aunty Anne's hands and Billy took the other. And instead of walking home they turned back down the street.

It's almost impossible to know if it was Aunty Anne who led them into the first sweetshop they came to or if it was the other way around.

About the Author

NICHOLAS ALLAN published his first book, *The Hefty Fairy*, in 1989. Since then he has written and illustrated over thirty books for children, including the bestselling picture books *The Queen's Knickers* and *Father Christmas Needs a Wee*. His books have won awards and been translated into twenty languages. Nicholas is also the author of *Hilltop Hospital*, a book that has been adapted into a BAFTA-winning television series for CITV and shown in over forty countries. He lives in London.

It takes a monster to know a monster!

Frank the big fat smelly ogre has come to Monster Hospital with a tummy ache. Join Sylvie, Dylan, Carolyn and Tom as they play doctor and see if they can help Frank without getting gobbled up or suffocating from the stupendous stink!

'This is a book full of fun'
SUNDAY TIMES CHILDREN'S BOOK OF THE WEEK

www.hodderchildrens.co.uk

It takes a monster to know a monster!

Bartholomew the dragon has come to Monster Hospital.
He's got a terrible case of smoke inhalation! Join Sylvie, Dylan,
Carolyn and Tom as they play doctor and see if they can help
Bartholomew without getting cooked to a crisp!

'Every page bristles with manic energy'
INDEPENDENT ON SUNDAY

www.hodderchildrens.co.uk

It takes a monster to know a monster!

Yuki the Yodelling Yeti is found sobbing in the snow and must be saved to stop her heart from melting. Join Sylvie, Dylan, Carolyn and Tom as they play doctor and see if they can help Yuki before her shrieks deafen them and destroy Monster Hospital!

www.hodderchildrens.co.uk

Hodder
Children's
Books

It takes a monster to know a monster!

Tommy the one-eyed monster has arrived at Monster Hospital by helicopter. He's a football star, but he's hurt his eye! Join Sylvie, Dylan, Carolyn and Tom as they play doctor and see if they can help him get better - and find out how the accident happened?

www.hodderchildrens.co.uk

Hodder Children's Books

my Funny Family

CHRIS HIGGINS

my Funny Family

Illustrated by
Lee Wildish

Mattie is nine years old and she worries about everything, which isn't surprising. Because when you have a family as big and crazy as hers, there's always something to worry about! Will the seeds she's planted in the garden with her brothers and sisters grow into fruit and veg like everyone promised? Why does it seem as if Grandma doesn't like them sometimes? And what's wrong with Mum?

Read the first book in the hilarious and heart-warming young series about the chaotic life of the Butterfield family.

Also available as an ebook

www.chrishigginsthatsme.com

Hodder Children's Books

It's the summer holiday and the Butterfield family is going away to Cornwall. As usual, Mattie has plenty to worry about. What if she loses the luggage she's been put in charge of? What if someone falls over a cliff? And worst of all ... what if they've forgotten someone?

Read the second book in the hilarious and heart-warming *My Funny Family* series.

OPERATION ITCHY BUM

When Alistair's mum decides that she's going on a blind date with the teacher from hell, Burke the Jerk, Al's worst nightmare has come true. And when she tells him that they're going on holiday with her new man, Al's got to do something drastic.

He packs his bag of total destruction and heads off for the holiday of a lifetime ...

www.hodderchildrens.co.uk

Hodder Children's Books

PARANORMAN

Now a major motion picture

PARANORMAN

YOU DON'T BECOME A HERO BY BEING NORMAL

Elizabeth Cody Kimmel

A hilarious and spooky adventure
– now a major motion picture!

Norman isn't afraid of ghosts. They're his friends – pretty much the only friends he has. When a terrible witch's curse unleashes a horde of zombies on his home-town, Norman needs to keep his head. And stop the zombies chewing on his brains.

Not an easy job when you've just been grounded.

It's a race against time: can Norman beat the zombies and save the day?

h
Hodder
Children's
Books